Dino FC

THE VANISHING GOALIE

KEITH BRUMPTON

USBORNE

DINO FC LINE-UP

CYRIL STEGOSAURUS
FULLBACK

STEGGY STEGOCERAS
DEFENDER

PTERADONNA
GOALKEEPER

MARCUS DIPLODOCUS
DEFENDER

TERRY TRICERATOPS
MANAGER / FULLBACK

ARCHIE OPTERYX
LEFT WINGER

ALBERT ALLOSAURUS
CENTRE MIDFIELD

CELIA COELOPHYSIS
FORWARD

GWEN CORYTHOSAURUS
CENTRE MIDFIELD

JOSÉ HETERODONTOSAURUS
FORWARD

ERIC ALLOSAURUS
RIGHT MIDFIELD

TODAY'S SUB:

OLLIE OVIRAPTOR
FORWARD

Go to www.keithbrumpton.co.uk
for more on Terry and the team.

First published in 2010 by Usborne Publishing Ltd., Usborne House,
83-85 Saffron Hill, London EC1N 8RT, England.
www.usborne.com

JFMAMJJA OND/10 00437/1 ISBN 9781409504863
Printed in Reading, Berkshire, UK.

Cup fever was in the air. Pteradonna, Dino FC's brilliant young goalie, and Celia Coelophysis, the speedy forward, could both feel it as they made their way to the club's training ground.

I'M SO EXCITED I CAN HARDLY WAIT FOR KICK-OFF.

ME NEITHER.

As they jogged past the Primeval Swamp, a couple of young dinosaurs stopped them and asked for their autographs.

The two players were very excited. Dino FC didn't have many fans and it had been quite a while since they'd been asked for a signature. It took Celia a while to get hers just right.

One of the fans was a young iguanodon called Iqbal.

GOOD LUCK WITH THE BIG GAME.

Thanks to Terry Triceratops's clever management and some cliffhanger victories, Dino FC had reached the final of the Dinosaur Football Association Cup and it seemed everyone knew about it.

SPORTING REPTIL

THE EVENING VOLCANO

TERRY'S BATTLERS!!!

DINO MAKE HISTORY!!

FINAL AT LAST

SOC

final app

Wannabe celebrity, Celia, was especially excited. If the team won there'd be lots of publicity. She might even get on the telly. Of course, she'd have to make sure she looked good – that meant claw varnish, make-up, and a new tracksuit!

MEET OUR SPECIAL GUEST, DINO FC'S CELIA COELOPHYSIS.

Pteradonna was more thrilled about the chance to show how brilliant she was in goal. She was a very dedicated young player and this was just the sort of occasion she'd been practising for.

At the club's training pitch, manager
Terry Triceratops wasn't looking quite as
happy as Celia and Pteradonna.

"Why the long face, boss?" asked his
loyal vice captain, Cyril Stegosaurus.

WE'RE IN A FINAL FOR
THE FIRST TIME EVER!

"That's great, I know..." Terry frowned, "...but I'm worried we've such a small squad."

"Small?" Cyril looked puzzled.

"No, I didn't mean that kind of small." Terry smiled. "I mean we don't have many players. With Ollie Oviraptor injured at the moment, there are only eleven of us."

Tough-tackling defender, Steggy Stegoceras, always enjoyed contradicting his manager.

"Yes, but what if someone else gets injured?" continued Terry. "Then we wouldn't even have anyone on the bench as sub."

"You worry too much," Steggy snorted, "these guys are hardened professionals."

Terry nodded. Maybe Steggy was right.

While Terry was fretting, Cyril got out some fossil cones for training. "A bit of training will be just the thing to keep the guys in tip-top condition!"

Marcus Diplodocus was warming up when he failed to spot a leaf on the wet ground in front of him. He slipped on it, fought to keep his balance, lost the struggle and his long legs flew out from under him.

WHOAHH!!!

He landed with a thud that could be
heard several valleys away.

"This is exactly what I was worried
about," Terry shouted to Cyril as he helped
a shaky Marcus to his feet.

WHERE DOES
IT HURT?

"Er, it doesn't," answered Marcus.

"Oh no! He can't feel anything!" gasped Terry. "That's bad!"

CALL A DOCTOR!

"No... I mean I can't feel anything 'cos I'm fine," smiled Marcus.

"The useless lump is okay," growled Steggy. "Let's get training."

The Dino FC squad breathed a big sigh of relief and got ready for action.

"No... Stop!" Terry shouted, waving his

hoofs in the air. "No training today. I'm calling it off."

Steggy Stegoceras didn't look happy. "But we've only just started."

"I can't risk it," replied Terry, firmly. He turned to the whole squad. "I want you all to go home and take it easy until the final. Don't go out of doors and don't play any sport."

The whole squad looked disappointed. They loved their football. And now Terry was telling them they couldn't play.

"The boss is only being sensible," said Cyril, trying to soften the blow.

Steggy shook his bony head to show he didn't agree.

And so it was that the Dino FC players went home without doing any training, and then tried as best as they could to follow their manager's orders...

ALBERT AND ERIC ALLOSAURUS DECIDED TO DO A JIGSAW PUZZLE TOGETHER.

GWEN CORYTHOSAURUS DID SOME WEIGHT TRAINING IN HER HOME GYM.

PTERADONNA READ A BOOK ON GOALKEEPING.

It looked like Terry's plan would pay off and the team would stay injury free. But, in football, nothing is simple...

At home in his tree house Terry was trying to
read some scouting reports on Dino FC's cup-
final opponents – Tyrannosaurus Hotspur.

But he was still worried about the team
getting injured and couldn't concentrate.
Instead he decided to check that everyone
was following his instructions. With the mid-
afternoon sun just beginning to cool, he set
off down the road.

Terry's first port of call was the clump of trees where Eric and Albert Allosaurus lived. He was still quite a long way off when he saw a large cloud of dust and heard loud growls emerging from it.

Terry recognized those growls straight away. It was the Allosaurus brothers, and as usual they were fighting!

The row was over a missing piece from a jigsaw they were doing together.

Terry found the piece they were looking for, helped complete the puzzle, and stayed until the brothers had made up.

Next, Terry decided he had better check on Cyril Stegosaurus. Surely his loyal vice captain was being sensible?

No such luck! Terry arrived to find Cyril lying on the ground groaning. The team's fullback looked twice his usual size and his legs were waving helplessly in the air.

"Cyril, what is it?" cried Terry, helping his friend back onto his feet.

Cyril looked embarrassed. "So sorry, boss, but I got bored with no training to keep me occupied," he replied, in between groans.

"A little snack?" exclaimed Terry, suddenly noticing that the leaves had been stripped from every bush in view.

Cyril shrugged guiltily. "It started with a couple of nibbles but the bushes were so tasty I couldn't stop."

While Cyril promised not to eat anything else until his stomach had gone back to its usual size, a worried Terry hurried off to see what Gwen Corythosaurus had been up to. He remembered her saying something about weight training, and after what he'd just seen that sounded far too dangerous!

When Terry reached the clearing where Gwen lived there was no sign of her anywhere. Terry was worried. What had happened? She'd said she would train at home and Gwen was one of the most reliable members of his team. Suddenly there came a muffled cry.

Terry looked around. There was no sign of Gwen. Just a huge limestone boulder.

A talking boulder, thought Terry. *That's weird!*

Terry hurried to the rock and began trying to lift it. "What happened?" he asked.

"I was weight training with this boulder, but it turned out to be a bit too heavy."

It took Terry ages to shift the rock from on top of Gwen.

Terry decided that leaving his players to their own devices was just too risky. But what was he going to do with them? It was a tricky problem. He sat on Gwen's training boulder and wondered how best to keep his team safe for the big match...

After thinking hard, Terry sent a message by dragonfly-mail.

He'd decided it was best to have the team back where he could keep an eye on them, even if that did mean risking injury.

Eric and Albert had patched up their jigsaw quarrel, Cyril's stomach was back to its normal size and Gwen seemed none the worse for having been squashed under a rock (luckily she was tough).

The squad limbered up under Terry's watchful eye, did a few sprints, and then practised some set-piece moves.

Terry felt sure the team would get lots of free kicks in the final, because Tyrannosaurus Hotspur were a very physical team. They had received more red rocks for foul play than any other team in the competition.

One of their forwards had even been suspended for eating a linesman after an argument over an offside flag (he'd eaten that too).

As his team trained by the golden glow of the setting sun, Terry had no idea that a very large dinosaur was crouched out of sight in some bushes, watching them. The dinosaur's name was Alex McTeeth, and he was a tyrannosaurus – in fact he was the manager of Dino FC's cup final opponents.

McTeeth was there on a spying mission. His bulging, bloodshot eyes swivelled from side to side as he watched every move Dino FC made. His jaws dribbled with excitement at what he saw.

Mcteeth sometimes wore glasses thinking they made him look brainier.

In all the time McTeeth had been watching, Pteradonna had stopped every shot fired at her. Even a thunderbolt from José Heterodontosaurus, who had one of the hardest shots on the team.

McTeeth was ruthless (like most tyrannosauruses), and he would stop at nothing to make sure his team won the cup final. As he watched Pteradonna performing so brilliantly, a plan formed in his head. It was an evil plan that might just mean the end of Dino FC's hopes of winning the final!

The team's training session came to an end as the first stars were spilling out across the prehistoric night sky.

   As the Dino FC squad made their way
home, chattering excitedly about the next
day's final, they passed by the very clump
of bushes where McTeeth had been hiding.
But now there was no one there. The
Tyrannosaurus Hotspur manager had
already left to put his evil scheme into action!

EXTRA! EXTRA! EXTRA!
DINO FC'S DAY OF DESTINY!

DINO
FIN
Special
Edition
Terry pre
open ga

Cup final day arrived. After a good night's
sleep, Pteradonna woke up, did some wing
stretches, ate a few small fish for breakfast
and then set out for an early morning flap.

Pteradonna was the youngest dinosaur in the Dino FC team, and this would be the biggest match she had ever played. But she still wasn't feeling nervous. Instead she said, "Bring it on."

It was a warm sunny day. Giant ferns waved in the breeze, dragonflies buzzed to and fro. Pteradonna flew from tree to tree, trying to catch the insects as she went – it was great practice for improving her goalie reactions.

Just as she was thinking of returning home to collect her kit, the young pterodactyl heard a twig snapping behind her. Something was rustling in the bushes and she thought she caught a glimpse of some very large white teeth.

But when she looked around there was no one there. "That's weird," she said, turning to fly off.

It was then that the ground beneath her gave way and Pteradonna fell into a deep, dark, narrow hole.

She hit the bottom of the hole with a thump some seconds later.

Pteradonna lay still for a few minutes, not moving. She was dazed and bruised but not badly injured.

I CAN FEEL MY CLAWS, THAT'S A GOOD SIGN. NOTHING BROKEN.

Then she looked up and saw two tyrannosaurus faces peering down at her.

"Hey! Did you leave this hole here?" she snapped at them, but they ignored her. She tried flapping her wings to fly back up again, but the hole was too narrow. She couldn't get off the ground.

"Nice work," said the first tyrannosaurus to the other.

AYE, MY PLAN HAS WORKED A TREAT...

"...She'll miss the game and we'll win the cup," chuckled the second, with an unpleasant sneer. Any Tyrannosaurus Hotspur fan would have known that face straight away. It belonged to their manager – Alex McTeeth!

Meanwhile, outside the Billennium Stadium, where the final would be played, fans were beginning to arrive, chattering eagerly about the game.

The Dino FC Squad had just arrived too, led by a worried-looking Terry.

"What's up, boss?" asked Cyril. He could always tell when his boss was troubled.

"It's Pteradonna," Terry answered. "It's not like her to be late. And no one has seen her all day. What if something's wrong and she doesn't turn up?"

WITHOUT HER WE DON'T STAND A CHANCE.

The rest of the team looked glum. They knew Pteradonna was always on time. Where could she be?

The rest of the team shook their heads in disagreement.

"She wouldn't miss this final for anything," said Celia, applying a pre-match mud pack to her face.

"There's nothing else for it," announced Terry, dramatically. "I'm going to go and look for her myself."

I KNOW THE SPOT IN THE FOREST WHERE SHE USUALLY TRAINS.

"What if you go missing as well?" groaned Ollie Oviraptor, thinking that Terry's pre-match plans were unravelling faster than a badly-knitted jumper.

"Yes," added Marcus Diplodocus, "and then we would only have, er…er…"

TEN PLAYERS, ONE OF WHOM IS AN OLD CROCK!

I'M NOT THAT OLD!

Ignoring the protests of his worried teammates, Terry was already on his way.

"If I'm not here for kick-off," he shouted back, "Cyril can take over as manager!"

TERRY SPRINTED OFF INTO THE FOREST, LEAVING A STUNNED AND WORRIED SQUAD BEHIND HIM.

Ollie Oviraptor offered to play in goal even though he was injured. It was a kind offer but creaky old Ollie could hardly stop a feather let alone a forward line of rampaging tyrannosauruses.

"Come on, it's time we found our dressing cave," said Cyril, trying to sound in control.

But deep down inside even he was worried.

Terry knew time was short. There was less than an hour till kick-off. He crashed through a group of spiky bushes, then used his three horns to clear a tangle of creepers that blocked his path, before swimming across an ophiderpeton-infested swamp!

Panting and out of breath, he climbed a large rock to get a better view of the forest beyond.

Who'd be a manager? thought Terry, looking down at the clump of trees where he knew Pteradonna trained. There was no sign of his missing goalie.

"Er, excuse me?" came a faint voice from the undergrowth beneath him.

The voice seemed to be coming from a large, spindly bush.

"Yes, that's me," answered Terry, carefully scrambling down from the rock.

"Great," came the reply, as a small iguanodon emerged nervously from the bush. It was Iqbal, the young Dino FC fan who'd asked for Celia and Pteradonna's autographs yesterday.

"I'm sorry, but I'm a bit busy," said Terry, seeing the autograph book in Iqbal's hand.

"No, this is very important," whispered the terrified youngster. He kept glancing around as if he expected something to leap out from the bushes at any moment.

"Okay, I'm listening. What's important?"

SSSH! KEEP YOUR VOICE DOWN! THEY'RE OUT THERE!

"Who?" asked Terry, starting to feel nervous himself. He sensed Iqbal was serious.

"Tyrannosauruses," came the reply. "Look, if you're searching for your goalie I know where she is," the young iguanodon whispered, still looking anxiously around him.

"What, Pteradonna?" gasped Terry, excitedly. "Where is she?" Maybe the match was not lost yet.

"Ssssh!" Iqbal hissed. "A giant tyrannosaurus has her trapped down a hole."

"A hole!" shrieked Terry in alarm.

Terry looked relieved. "So where is this hole?" he whispered.

Iqbal pointed back to the forest.

And so the young iguanodon cautiously led the way to the terrible tyrannosaurus's trap. The first thing Terry saw was the tyrannosaurus on guard. He wasn't hard to miss: ten metres of solid muscle; sharp teeth, lined up like a set of ivory cutlery, and beady eyes, alert for the slightest movement.

"How do we get to the hole with him there?" whispered Iqbal.

Terry pondered his options like the expert football manager he was. He could think of two.

1) Run away. Probable result: lose goalkeeper and lose the cup final.

2) Think of a plan to distract the tyrannosaurus. Probable result: unknown, but possibly very dangerous.

Terry knew he had to go for option two. Now all he needed to do was work out how to get the tyrannosaurus's attention away from the hole.

Terry found himself a spot in the bushes
where the tyrannosaurus would be able to
hear him without seeing him. His heart was
racing faster than a sprinting Archie
Opteryx.

He had discovered a large, hollow coconut shell, and was holding it next to his mouth. Now he cast his mind back to when he had watched Alex McTeeth, Tyrannosaurus Hotspur's cheating manager, on "Big Match Live".

How had he spoken again? Terry deepened his voice by growling into the coconut shell.

Iqbal watched as the tyrannosaurus guarding the hole turned towards the voice that boomed out from the bushes.

The tyrannosaurus, who was not very bright and always hungry, peered down the hole one last time, then lumbered slowly away...

Moments later, Terry was peering down into the same deep, dark hole. To his relief, his young goalkeeper looked unharmed.

"Don't panic!" he called down into the darkness. "It's me, Terry…"

I'LL GET YOU OUT!

"Are we still in time for the final?" Pteradonna shouted back. She loved her football every bit as much as Terry did.

Terry couldn't answer her question. Time was hurrying by faster than a herd of apatosauruses down a steep slope.

He turned to Iqbal. "We need to get her out!"

BUT WHAT IF THAT TYRANNOSAURUS COMES BACK?

Terry knew the burly dinosaur was still a danger. "Okay, you keep watch while I concentrate on Pteradonna. If you see anything, yell out as loud as you can."

Iqbal nodded and took up a good viewing spot.

Meanwhile, Terry had no idea how he was going to free his young goalie from the tyrannosaurus's trap.

He thought hard. But he kept worrying that the DFA cup final was about to kick off without him and the team's star goalie. Terry tried to focus on the problem. And suddenly he came up with an idea. He  grabbed a long length of jungle creeper that was dangling close by, tore a length off, and then fed it down the hole towards Pteradonna. He tied one end to a large tree and tugged it hard to check it was secure.

OKAY, PTERADONNA, HAVE YOU GOT THE CREEPER?

YES!

GOOD, THEN SEE IF YOU CAN CLIMB UP!

If it had been any other member of the team there would have been no chance of the creeper bearing their weight, but Pteradonna was small and fairly light. The creeper looked like it would take her weight, but was she strong enough to climb all the way out of such a deep hole?

The rest of Dino FC had changed into their match kit and Cyril was trying to give a stirring team talk. But without Terry's leadership everything was in chaos and he struggled to make himself heard.

Eric and Albert were fighting over who would carry the practice ball.

Celia was looking for a missing false eyelash and Marcus had just discovered he'd left his shorts in the wash. "No one else will have my size," he groaned.

Cyril tried to make himself heard above the din. "We're going to play 4–2–4," he shouted.

"But there are only ten of us in the team and that's including Ollie in goal," pointed out Steggy, grumpily. He was still cross that he hadn't been made manager while Terry was away.

"Er, 4–1–4 then," tried Cyril. But he had no idea how this formation would work.

"Terry isn't going to get back in time," fretted Ollie, gloomily.

No one felt like contradicting him. The atmosphere in the Dino FC dressing room was very downbeat. What could possibly stop Tyrannosaurus Hotspur from winning the cup?

Deep in the jungle, young Pteradonna, her claws wrapped around the creeper, was still trying to climb up the final stretch of the hole. The tree bent with her weight. The creeper twisted and looked like it might snap.

Terry mopped his brow. Higher and higher she climbed.

Iqbal was still keeping watch – and listening hard for approaching footsteps, or a deep-throated growl.

Suddenly he heard the sound he'd been dreading: heavy tyrannosaurus footsteps. Every dinosaur knew that noise – and every dinosaur feared it!

After what seemed an age, Pteradonna's claws finally appeared out of the hole, followed slowly by her head, body, folded wings and tail.

Exhausted, she scrambled out of the hole into the bright sunlight and lay flat out in a clump of ferns. "Thanks, guys, thanks..." she puffed.

From the woods, the footsteps were drawing closer. And now bushes and leaves were rustling too as they were trampled on and brushed aside. But Pteradonna wasn't thinking about the danger. Her thoughts were already focused on the cup final.

THE MATCH WILL BE STARTING ANY MINUTE NOW. WE'D BETTER FLY.

ER, I CAN'T. TRICERATOPS CAN'T FLY. YOU GO AHEAD — I'LL FOLLOW AS QUICKLY AS I CAN.

WHAT ABOUT THE TYRANNOSAURUS GUARD?

"We can outrun him," answered Terry, trying to convince himself as well as his young goalie.

Pteradonna gave Terry a worried look, but then she nodded her long pointy head. She showed Terry a short cut through the forest that would help him escape. Then, without delay, she flapped off, up above the trees and into a clear blue sky. Like most pteranodons she didn't fly gracefully but she did fly fast. It wouldn't take long to reach the Billennium Stadium.

"We need to get to the final too," said Terry to Iqbal. "And that tyrannosaurus is getting closer! Come on!"

"The final?" said the surprised iguanodon. "But I don't have a ticket."

I'LL SORT THAT. YOU'LL BE MY SPECIAL GUEST.

And they ran off, following Pteradonna's short cut, hoping they could shake off the pursuing tyrannosaurus en route.

Meanwhile, Pteradonna was making good progress, flapping as hard as she could and with a helpful tailwind blowing her towards the stadium. Already she could see the two opposing teams in the distance, warming up.

Terry raced through the forest, at top speed. He charged through the long grass, crashed through bushes and flattened anything in his path – even trees! Young Iqbal was close behind, trying to keep up.

The Billennium Stadium.

With just seconds to go before kick-off, Pteradonna landed on the pitch, and was mobbed by her delighted teammates. It was like she'd saved a penalty.

Pteradonna quickly told them the whole story.

"Those cheating tyrannosauruses," growled Eric Allosaurus, when he heard about the trap and Terry's dramatic rescue. For once his brother Albert agreed with him.

Watching the scene of Pteradonna's unexpected arrival, Alex McTeeth and his Tyrannosaurus team couldn't believe their shifty, twitching eyes. How on earth had the Dino FC goalie escaped their trap?

The referee blew his nose as a signal to start the DFA cup final.

Up in their commentary box, the experts were puzzled by Terry's absence.

AND IT MEANS OF COURSE THAT ERIC ALLOSAURUS IS HAVING TO FILL IN AT RIGHT BACK...

AND HE'S NOT A RIGHT BACK. NO WAY IS HE A RIGHT BACK.

THE GUY IS NOT A DEFENDER, GARY, AND HOTSPUR WILL PROBE DOWN THAT FLANK, MARK MY WORDS.

"What words?" asked Gary Seymouria who had a very short memory. For once the DBC (Dinosaur Broadcasting Corporation) experts were right in their analysis. Straight from the kick-off, Tyrannosaurus Hotspur attacked down Dino FC's right wing. But they found Eric Allosaurus in a determined mood. His brother Albert had told him he would make a rubbish fullback and Eric was desperate to prove him wrong.

He made tackle after tackle and Tyrannosaurus Hotspur soon began to get frustrated. They were playing against a weakened Dino FC with poor old Ollie not fit enough to play, but *still* they couldn't score.

So, like the mean, crooked team they were they changed tactics and began cheating. They threatened the ref.

And they fouled and pulled shirts and rolled on the ground every time they were tackled.

Cyril Stegosaurus really wished Terry was there to help the team out.

Thirty minutes into the game a Tyrannosaurus Hotspur player clearly handled the ball. But the ref said nothing. He was too frightened to blow for a free kick. Instead the Hotspur forward carried on through an astonished Dino FC defence and smashed the ball past Pteradonna. Or at least it looked as if he had. The flying goalkeeper took off, twisted in mid-air, and pushed the ball up and over the crossbar.

It was an amazing save.

Hotspur took a corner. A powerful header came whizzing towards the net.

It should have been a goal, but somehow Pteradonna managed to claw it away.

From then on Pteradonna made a whole string of acrobatic saves to keep her team in the game.

The Dino FC fans were still on their feet cheering Pteradonna when the ref blew his nose for half-time. Somehow a patched-up Dino FC had made it through the forty-five gruelling minutes with their goal intact and the scoreline still blank: nil-nil!

As Dino FC sat in their dressing cave,
exhausted by their efforts, the players were
expecting another of Cyril's boring team
talks. But before Cyril could open his mouth
to speak, a familiar triceratops came
hurrying into the cave. It was Terry!

"Okay, team, the scoreboard says nil-nil,
so we've still got a great chance to win this
game," he announced, out of breath after his
run through the forest, but full of enthusiasm.

"Ollie, you've done brilliantly, but I'll take your place now. Eric, you can go back into midfield. I've got a hunch Tyrannosaurus Hotspur aren't as fit as we are, so they'll be feeling tired. Let's use our nippy wingers – Celia and Archie – to get in behind them."

The team nodded.
It made good sense.

AND THEY'RE A BIG, TALL SIDE, SO LET'S KEEP THE BALL ON THE GROUND WITH LOTS OF LITTLE PASSES...

The team were ready to carry out Terry's instructions to the letter. They were still angry at how their opponents had tried to cheat at every opportunity.

As Dino FC ran back onto the pitch their gigantic opponents were already waiting, teeth bared, jagged claws glinting in the sunlight. But Dino FC weren't intimidated.

They were more determined than ever
that the cheating tyrannosauruses would not
win.

The second half started with another
classic save by Pteradonna. She remembered
Terry's instructions and, instead of kicking
the ball in the air, she threw it in a long
curving arc, straight to Archie's feet.

Archie set off on a weaving run, jinking
from side to side, which is what he was good
at. The tired tyrannosauruses were slow to

react. Archie escaped three lunging tackles, then hit a perfect pass through to lightning-fast Celia, who struck the ball first time – right into the back of the net.

CHAPTER 12

Alex McTeeth roared angrily at his team.

COME ON, YOU USELESS HUNKS OF BLUBBER! GET STUCK IN!

He hated losing. But criticizing and roaring at his team only served to make the players more nervous. Minutes later, José Heterodontosaurus used his wily skills to dink the ball through to Archie Opteryx, who shot from the edge of the box.

The Dino fans couldn't believe it. They'd never imagined they could take the lead against such a huge side. Iqbal waved his scarf proudly in the air, knowing he'd played his part.

But the scoring wasn't over yet. Alex McTeeth was sent to the stands for deliberately terrifying a linesman and the rest of his team were beginning to look more and more tired.

As Tyrannosaurus Hotspur's tails drooped, Terry set off on a mazy dribble of his own. He played a crisp one-two with Gwen, and smashed the ball home!

THAT'S HIS BEST OF THE SEASON!

WHAT A BEAUTY!

It was now three-nil, and even though the terrified referee was "persuaded" by Hotspur's players to add on ten minutes of fictional injury time, Dino FC held on...

SOME DINOSAURS ARE ON THE PITCH, GARY...THEY THINK IT'S ALL OVER!

But, of course, it wasn't just the game they won, Dino FC were the winners of the DFA Cup. It was their first trophy for a million years. Not only that, but Pteradonna won the Dinosaur of the Match Award for her amazing performance in the first half.

The team held up their trophy, then they lifted up their manager. From Eric and Albert's shoulders an excited Terry Triceratops turned to the team's fans.

THIS WIN IS DEDICATED TO DINO FC'S MOST LOYAL FAN – IQBAL IGUANODON!

As Terry described how Iqbal had come to their rescue, the young iguanadon's green face turned pink with embarrassment and pride.

Terry couldn't wait for the next match. Now they'd won their first trophy he was sure his team of likeable misfits were ready for anything!

THE END

CLAWNOTE: TYRANNOSAURUS HOTSPUR MANAGER ALEX MCTEETH LATER RECEIVED A THREE-MATCH BAN FOR ATTEMPTING TO EAT THE REFEREE IN THE PLAYERS' TUNNEL. IN A PRESS CONFERENCE HE CLAIMED HIS TEAM HAD BEEN "ROBBED".

MEET THE PLAYERS IN DINO FC

– THE CRAZIEST TEAM IN THE JURASSIC WORLD!

RUMBLEY STADIUM - THE DINO FC GROUND

PTERADONNA

1

POSITION: goalkeeper

SKILLS: flying

LIKES: catching crosses

DISLIKES: non-football days

FOOTY FACT: the youngest member of the squad

STEGGY STEGOCERAS

2

POSITION: defender

SKILLS: good at marking opponents

LIKES: grumbling

DISLIKES: being told what to do

FOOTY FACT: applied for the manager's job but Terry got it

MARCUS DIPLODOCUS

3

POSITION: defender

SKILLS: great in the air

LIKES: heading the ball

DISLIKES: quick forwards

FOOTY FACT: last season won 76% of all headers

TERRY TRICERATOPS

4

POSITION: manager and fullback

SKILLS: tactician

LIKES: tough talking

DISLIKES: defensive football

FOOTY FACT: only player-manager in the DPL

CYRIL STEGOSAURUS

5

POSITION: fullback

SKILLS: following instructions

LIKES: moving slowly

DISLIKES: anyone criticizing Terry, "the boss"

FOOTY FACT: the vice-captain

ALBERT ALLOSAURUS

6

POSITION: midfield

SKILLS: dealing with tricky forwards

LIKES: arguing with his twin

DISLIKES: Eric. Refs

FOOTY FACT: once got 21 red cards in a season

GWEN CORYTHOSAURUS

7

POSITION: midfield

SKILLS: controlling midfield

LIKES: playing in the rain

DISLIKES: hot temperatures

FOOTY FACT: the team's free kick specialist

ARCHIE OPTERYX

8

POSITION: winger

SKILLS: great dribbler

LIKES: doing ball tricks

DISLIKES: bumpy pitches

FOOTY FACT: takes the team's corners

ERIC ALLOSAURUS

9

POSITION: midfield
SKILLS: tackling, marking
LIKES: arguing with his twin
DISLIKES: Albert. Refs
FOOTY FACT: once got 20 red cards in a season

CELIA COELOPHYSIS

10

POSITION: forward
SKILLS: fast and graceful
LIKES: looking good on the pitch
DISLIKES: tackling or being tackled
FOOTY FACT: fastest player on the team

JOSÉ HETERODONTOSAURUS

11

POSITION: forward
SKILLS: falling over in the box
LIKES: winning penalties
DISLIKES: most things
FOOTY FACT: on average only fit for 2.3 games per season

OLLIE OVIRAPTOR

12

POSITION: utility player
SKILLS: football brain, experience
LIKES: resting after the match
DISLIKES: playing 90 minutes
FOOTY FACT: has been a pro for 22 seasons

CHECK OUT MORE CRAZY FOOTY ACTION IN:

9781409504832

9781409504856

9781409504849

For more action-packed reads head to